P9-DCP-501

# Bailey
# Goes Camping

## By Kevin Henkes

Greenwillow Books  New York

# FOR LAURA

Library of Congress
Cataloging in Publication Data

Henkes, Kevin.
Bailey goes camping.
Summary: Bailey is too young to
go camping with the Bunny Scouts,
but his parents take him on a
special camping trip—in the house.
1. Children's stories, American.
[1. Camping—Fiction.
2. Rabbits—Fiction]     I. Title.
PZ7.H389Bai 1985
[E]     84-29027
ISBN 0-688-05701-2
ISBN 0-688-05702-0 (lib. ed.)

Bruce and Betty were Bunny Scouts.

They were going camping.

Bailey had to stay home.

"I want to go camping," said Bailey.

"You're too little to go," said Bruce.

"But in a few years you can," said Betty.

"Don't feel bad, Bailey," said Bruce. "It's not *that* great. All we do is eat hot dogs and live in a tent and go swimming and fishing and hunt for bears and tell ghost stories and fall asleep under the stars."

"And don't forget roasting marshmallows," said Betty. "That's best of all!"

Bailey watched Bruce and Betty leave.

"It's not fair," he said.

"Come on," said Papa, "let's play baseball."

"No," said Bailey.

"Want to help me bake cookies?" said Mama.

"No," said Bailey.

"We could read a book," said Papa.

"No," said Bailey. "I want to go camping."

"You're too little to go," said Papa.

"But in a few years you can," said Mama.

"Don't feel bad, Bailey," said Papa. "It's not
   *that* great."
"Oh, yes, it is," said Bailey. "You get to eat
   hot dogs and live in a tent and go
   swimming and fishing and hunt for
   bears and tell ghost stories and fall asleep
   under the stars. And best of all, you roast
   marshmallows."

"You know," said Mama, "you can do
all those things right here."

"I *can*?" said Bailey.

"He *can*?" said Papa.

"Yes," said Mama, smiling.

That afternoon, Bailey ate hot dogs

and lived in a tent.

He went swimming

and fishing.

That night, Bailey went on a bear hunt

and told ghost stories.

And best of all,

he roasted marshmallows—

before falling asleep
under the stars.